AF153996

Nova Scotia Railway

Rules and Regulations to be Observed by the Officers and Men in the Service of the Board of Commissioners

SALZWASSER
VERLAG

Nova Scotia Railway

Rules and Regulations to be Observed by the Officers and Men in the Service of the Board of Commissioners

Reprint of the original, first published in 1859.

1st Edition 2022 | ISBN: 978-3-37513-192-0

Verlag (Publisher): Salzwasser Verlag GmbH, Zeilweg 44, 60439 Frankfurt, Deutschland
Vertretungsberechtigt (Authorized to represent): E. Roepke, Zeilweg 44, 60439 Frankfurt, Deutschland
Druck (Print): Books on Demand GmbH, In de Tarpen 42, 22848 Norderstedt, Deutschland

NOVA SCOTIA RAILWAY.

RULES AND REGULATIONS

TO BE OBSERVED BY THE

OFFICERS AND MEN

IN THE SERVICE OF

THE BOARD OF COMMISSIONERS.

RAILWAY OFFICE,
APRIL, 1859.

INDEX.

		Page
Act authorizing Board of Commissioners to make regulations		5
Section 1.	General Regulations	7
2.	Signals	12
3.	Running of Trains	14
4.	Station Master	19
5.	Conductor	23
6.	Engine Drivers	29
7.	Brakemen	36
8.	Baggage Masters	38
9.	Firemen	39
10.	Mechanics and others	39
11.	Switchmen	42
12.	Roadmaster	43
13.	Private Road crossings	47
14.	Penalties	48
15.	Regulations in regard to Passsengers	48
16.	In regard to Baggage	49
17.	General Notices & Conditions of Carriage.	50
	Act for the regulation of Railways	57

NOVA SCOTIA RAILWAY.

RULES AND REGULATIONS.

An Act to authorize the Board of Commissioners to make Regulations for the construction and management of Railways in Nova Scotia.

(Passed the 31st day of March, 1855.)

Be it enacted by the Governor, Council and Assembly as follows:

The Board of Commissioners of Railways in this province, are hereby authorized to make regulations from time to time for the safe construction and working of the railways under their charge,—for the transmission of goods and passengers thereon,—for their care and management, and that of the plant and equipment used thereon,—for the protection of the wharves, bridges, culverts, crossings, stations, buildings, and depots erected or to be erected, and all other the property in the possession and under the control of the Board in their public capacity. And in such regulations to affix fines, penalties and punishments for the breach thereof. Provided always that such regulations before going into operation shall be first sanctioned by the Governor in Council.

The Governor in Council. shall have power by order for that purpose made, to except from drill, training or other militia service all persons engaged in the actual construction of railways in this province.

NOTICE.

It shall be encumbent upon every person employed upon the railway, to have in his possession the rules and regulations herein set forth, or that may from time to time be issued, and to be conversant with them, not only to the extent of the duties applicable to his own particular position, but generally as required from all classes engaged on the line.

REGULATIONS

MADE UNDER AND BY VIRTUE OF AN ACT ENTITLED

"An Act to authorize the Board of Commissioners to make Regulations for the Construction and Management of Railways in Nova-Scotia."

Passed in the 18th Year of Her present Majesty's reign.

SECTION FIRST.

General Regulations.

1.   EACH person employed in the Railway service is to devote himself exclusively to that service, attending during the prescribed hours of the day or night, and residing wherever he may be required by those in authority over him.

2. He must *obey promptly* all instructions he may receive from persons placed in authority over him, and conform to all the regulations of the Commissioners.

3. He will be liable to immediate dismissal for disobedience of orders, negligence, incompetency, using improper language, intoxication, or incivility to passengers.

4. Unless appointed so to do, he is on no occasion, nor under any pretence whatever, to receive money from any person on the Commissioners' account.

5. No person is allowed under any circumstances to absent himself from duty without the permission of the head of the department in which he may be employed, except in case of illness, and then notice is to be immediately sent to his superior officer.

6. No person is to quit the Railway service without giving fourteen days previous notice to the Superintendent, and in case he leave without such notice, all pay then due will be forfeited.

7. The Commissioners reserve the right to deduct from the pay of each person employed in the service, such sums as may be awarded against him for neglect of duty as fines.

8. Each person is expected, when on duty, to appear in an efficient and proper state of cleanliness and neatness, and to take good care of any clothing which may have been supplied

to him by the Commissioners. Any person on leaving the Railway service must at once deliver up to his immediate superior all property entrusted to his care.

If any such property shall have been improperly used or damaged, a deduction from the pay due shall be made, sufficient to make good the damage or to supply new articles.

9. *Intemperance* being a vice which brings in its train every species of crime, and which, on a Railway, leads to the most fearful accidents, *all parties* employed by the Commissioners are *strictly prohibited* from *drinking any spirituous liquors when on duty*, and from carrying any with them for the use of others. Any man in the Railway service found *intoxicated either on or off duty, will be immediately dismissed*, it being indispensable that only men of strictly temperate habits be employed where the safety of life and property is concerned.

10. All persons employed in the Railway service are strictly forbidden from entering into *altercation* with any other person, whatever provocation may have been given; they will make a note of the facts if necessary, and report to their immediate superior.

11. All persons in places of trust in the Railway service must report any misconduct or negligence affecting the interest or safety of the road, which may come within their knowledge: and their withholding any such information will be considered a proof of neglect and indifference on their part.

12.   All employes of the Railway are expected and required in all cases to exercise the *greatest care and watchfulness* to prevent injury or damage to persons or property, and in doubtful cases to take the safe side.

13.   Each person will be held legally liable for injury occasioned to persons or property by his negligence.

14.   The pay of every man *absent* or *suspended* from duty will be stopped. No persons are allowed to receive gratuities.

15.   In all cases where *instructions* may *not* be *understood*, or where the course to be pursued admits of any doubt, the parties in charge shall so act as in no way to compromise the safety of the road, seeking afterwards, with the first opportunity, the necessary explanations of the proper officers.

Every person is required to give the *strictest attention* to the *danger* and *caution* signals. He is not to judge of the necessity of any signal shown ; the responsibility of giving them rests with those who exhibit them, and it is indispensable that they be *implicitly obeyed.*

16.   The Chronometer at Richmond Station is the *standard* of time for the whole road.

Station Masters, Conductors, and Road Masters, will be held responsible for always keeping their time-pieces to the *true* time, which, until the telegraph be erected, Station Masters will receive daily from the Guards. The importance of having correct time kept by all parties can not be too strongly insisted on.

17. Each officer shall make himself thoroughly acquainted with all Time-Tables and Special Rules which may be made from time to time, and shall keep a copy of the same on his person when on duty, as well as a copy of these Regulations, under a penalty of ten shillings for each neglect.

18. Each Conductor, Baggage Master, and Brakeman, while on duty, shall wear upon his hat or cap a badge which shall indicate his office.

19. Each officer or employe of the Railway is prohibited from smoking while on duty in the cars, stations, or depots.

20. They are also strictly forbidden from taking charge of any letters or parcels uninvoiced, except those belonging exclusively to the Railway service.

21. Employes disapproving of these Regulations, or not disposed to aid in carrying them out, are requested not to remain in the Railway service.

SECTION SECOND.

—

Signals.

22. RED is a signal of *danger.—Stop.*

GREEN.—*Caution. Proceed slowly, not exceeding five miles an hour.*

WHITE.—*All right. Go on.*

These Signals will be made by *Flags* in the day-time, and by *Lamps* at night.

In addition to this, *any* Signal waved *violently*, or a man standing with both arms raised above his head, denotes danger, and the necessity of stopping immediately.

23. The red flag is the flag of danger whenever displayed. At road crossings, when displayed across the common road, it signifies that the train is coming, and travellers must look out. But whenever a *red* flag or *red* light is displayed *on* the track, it signifies danger to the train, *and the train must stop*, and ascertain the cause of the danger.

24. These Signals shall always be shown on the *right hand* side of the Engine-driver of the approaching train.

25. Engines with passenger trains must carry one *white* light in front, after sunset. Every train or empty engine moving on the line after sunset, shall display one or more *red* tail lights.

26. The Conductor of the train is responsible for attaching the tail lamp on the last car, and the Engine-driver and Fireman for placing the lamp on the engine or tender. When a car is detached care must be taken to see that the tail light is removed and re-attached to the train.

27. The tail signal must be inspected at every station; and in the event of the train being brought to a stand on the main line, from any cause, the Conductor must take care that no one stands before the tail lamp so as to prevent its being seen.

28. A red flag by day, or two red lights by night, hung at the back of the train, or in front of an engine, denotes that an EXTRA TRAIN is to follow, for which freight, ballast, or wood trains MUST WAIT.

29. Two sounds of the whistle is the Signal to apply the brakes.

ONE sound of the whistle to let go the brakes.

THREE sounds of the whistle is the Signal for backing the train.

FOUR sounds of the whistle is a Signal of recall to Flagmen.

30. The bell is always to be sounded when approaching a level crossing or station.

31. The whistle is to be sounded (being careful to avoid frightening horses) with a con-

tinuous sound half a mile before reaching any · station or level crossing of a public road.

32. The bell must be rung from one-quarter of a mile before reaching any level crossing of a public road, until the crossing be passed.

33 Frequent use of the whistle must always be made in foggy weather, and in snow-storms.

34. No one can be allowed to judge of a *danger* or *caution* Signal, EXCEPT THE ONE BY WHOM IT IS GIVEN. *All signals must be obeyed.*

35. Signal cords shall be used on all trains, and shall extend from the rear car to the whistle or alarm bell on the engine.

SECTION THIRD.

Running of Trains.

36. Trains shall be classed as :
 1st. — Regular Passenger Trains ;
 2d. — Special Trains ;
 3d. — Freight Trains ;
 4th. — Ballast or Wood Trains.

37. All trains of an INFERIOR class must *keep out of the way* of all trains of a SUPERIOR class going in either direction.

38. All regular passenger trains will leave termini at the specified time, and *trains due must keep clear.*

39. If any part of a train is detached when in motion, care must be taken not to stop the train in front before the detached part has stopped, and the Conductor of such a detached part must apply his brake in time to prevent a collision with the cars in front, in the event of their stopping.

40. No special train or engine shall be despatched from any station without the direct authority of the Superintendent.

41. No train must leave an intermediate station when another train is due, until such train arrives, or positive instructions in writing or by telegraph are received from the Superintendent or Conductor, that the expected train will not come. Whenever telegraph despatches are used for the movement of trains, they must, in all cases, be repeated back from the receiving office to the sending office, and acknowledged before the Conductor starts his train, and then proceed with care. All such orders must be given in writing by the Telegraph Agent to the Conductor or to the Engine-driver, before starting.

42. Regular passenger trains will not wait for freight trains. Freight trains must be on a siding FIFTEEN MINUTES at least before the regular time of passenger trains. Freight, ballast, and wood trains must also *wait in a siding for extra and special trains*, of which notice is given by signals, giving the extra or special trains the right to the road.

43. If any train breaks down or is delayed on the road, the *first duty* of all persons connected with the train is to see that every precaution is used to prevent any other train from running into the delayed train. ONE, and in cases of danger TWO efficient men, must be sent *backwards and forwards*, with red flags or lamps, at least half a mile, to stop any approaching train. No wish to have the Signalmen go on in the delayed train must prevent their going back at least half a mile, and stopping until the approaching train is stopped; and if a third or fourth train is following, the same precaution must be observed. THIS RULE IS OF THE UTMOST IMPORTANCE.

44. No engine or train must leave or pass a station within fifteen minutes of another, going in the same direction.

45. Whenever it becomes necessary to back a train to a station, it must be done with great care, keeping at least two men with red flags or red lights, constantly in advance of the rear end of the train, to warn any train that may be approaching. Neither the Conductor nor Engine-driver has a right to assume that there are no trains approaching in either direction.

46. Gravel and wood trains must be on a siding *twenty minutes* before a train is due, and *wait till all trains due have arrived.*

47. No extra or uncertain train will leave any station unless it has time to arrive at the

next station at least fifteen minutes before the time fixed in any Time-Table for the arrival of any regular train.

48. In the meeting of trains at the stations. each train must take the left-hand track, excepting uncertain trains, which must take the siding. and must remain until the expected train arrives.

49. If any uncertainty arise as to the entire safety of proceeding with the train, a signal must be sent backward or forward, as the case may be, and be kept at least half a mile distant from the train, until the danger is over.

50. Trains following each other must keep three miles apart.

51. An extra or special train following a regular train, will approach all stations and wooding places with great care, expecting to find the preceding train taking wood or water at such station, whether it may be a stopping place for that train or not. The responsibility of a collision will rest upon the Conductor and Engine-driver of the special train.

52. Gravel and wood trains shall DAILY, before leaving their stations for the day's work, report to the Superintendent, and also leave with the Station-Master a memorandum of where the train will be working for the day, and such memorandum shall be entered by the Station-Master in a book to be kept for that purpose.

This book shall be open to the inspection of all persons on duty connected with the trains.

53. Red flags or red lamps must always be placed at a safe distance on either side of the ground where gravel trains are at work, and a man must remain with them. The same precautions must be used when single cars are at work on the road, when repairs of bridges are going on, or any description of repairs which interfere with the safety of the track.

54. Torpedoes must be carried upon every train, to be used as follows: Should the train be detained from any cause during the night, or by fogs or storms of snow or rain during the day, in such a position as to endanger a following or approaching train, in addition to all other precautions TWO TORPEDOES must be tied—one upon each rail, at a distance of 800 yards, and all trains *must stop* as soon as possible after the explosion of a torpedo, without waiting for other signals.

55. No ballast or wood train, and no hand car or trolly is allowed to be on the main line during a fog or snow storm, unless under the especial order of the Superintendent.

56. Whenever it shall be necessary to send a special engine over the road a-head of any regular train, it shall run on its time and shall be entitled to its rights, and shall carry the proper signals for the regular train which follows.

57. The rear car of every train must be a *brake car*, and a man must, when the train is in motion, be always stationed on that car.

58. When trains are to *pass each other*, the train having the right to the road shall occupy the main track.

59. No *verbal message* touching the safety of trains, track, or bridges, *must be sent* or *received*, except in cases of pressing necessity.— Such messages should be sent in writing to prevent misconstruction.

60. In forming a passenger train, baggage, freight, or lumber cars *shall not* be placed in rear of the passenger cars.

61. Engines and cars must in no case be left upon the main track. They must be placed as quickly as possible *in a siding*, clear of the main line, WITH THE WHEELS SCOTCHED. At night the first car must be chained and locked.

SECTION FOURTH.

Station Master.

62. He is responsible for the proper use and care of all the buildings and property of the Railway, and is answerable for the faithful and efficient discharge of the duties of all persons employed at his station.

63. He must see that all *orders* are *duly executed*, and that all books and returns are regularly written up and neatly kept.

64. He must see that all servants at the station behave respectfully and civilly to passengers of every class.

65. He must inspect *daily* all rooms and places in connection with the station, and see that they are kept neat and clean.

66. He must see that all stores supplied for the station are prudently and economically used, and that there is *no waste* of oil, fuel, or stationery.

67. He is not to be *absent without leave* from the Superintendent, except from illness, in which case he must immediately inform the Superintendent and take care that some competent person is entrusted with his duties.

68. He is required to see that *every article* loaded in the cars, is entered on the freight forwarded book and on the invoice, and also that every article so entered on the invoice is actually loaded in the car designated thereon.

69. He is held *personally responsible* for the safe keeping and proper delivery of all *goods* received by him, and for *all charges* due thereon ; and all articles mentioned upon the invoices will be considered as having been received by the agent at the destined station, and in good order;

unless otherwise stated by him on the face of the invoice.

70. He will *report* immediately to the superintendent whenever any train leaves his station *before* the *time* prescribed in the time tables.

71. He will have charge of the switchmen at the station. He will be held strictly responsible for the position of all *switches* at the station, and must always assume that *at any moment* a train may be expected. *Switches* must always be right for the *main line*, excepting when immediately being used.

72. He will make separate *invoices* of the contents of *each car*, and also of freight destined to different stations. Every loaded freight car must be accompanied by an invoice showing its freight and destination.

73. He is to report, WITHOUT DELAY, neglect of duty on the part of any one under his charge; and in case of complaint against any man, he is to communicate the particulars as soon as possible, so that the offender may be sent to head quarters if the case require it.

74. He will be responsible for all money received at his station, and will be required to make good any deficiency. He must make up and balance his accounts daily.

75. He must take care that no parcels or packages whatever are transmitted by the rail-

2

way WITHOUT BEING DULY ENTERED and the carriage paid or charged.

76.   He must not supply or lend, under any pretence or circumstances, stores or any other articles belonging to the railway.

77.   The train is under the direction of the station master so long as it remains at his station.

78.   He will direct the conductor of each train when to start, and use every exertion to ensure punctuality in its departure. He will not allow any train to pass his station within fifteen minutes of a former train going in the same direction.

79.   In case of accident to any train on the road he will, on receiving information thereof, act according to circumstances in such a way as to give the earliest assistance, and prevent as much as possible any subsequent detention.

80.   After the passage of trains he will see that everything about the station is safe from fire.

81.   In case of any injury to the track coming to his knowledge, he will immediately despatch some person to notify the track repairers, and see that it is repaired; and in case the track repairers are not at hand employ others to do it, and take measures, if necessary, to warn coming trains.

SECTION FIFTH.

Conductor.

82.   The Conductor will have *entire charge* and control *of the train,* and all persons employed on it, and is responsible for its movements while on the road, except when his directions conflict with these *regulations,* or involve any risk or hazard, in either of which cases, all participating will be held accountable.

83.   He must *see* that the *regulations* are *observed* by those under him, and report, daily, to the Superintendent, all violations of them.

84.   He must be in attendance one hour before starting his *train* from any terminal station, and see that his cars are *clean,* and in *good* and *safe* order, particularly examining the *wheels, axles, brakes,* and *springs,* and while on the road that the routine duties of those employed on the trains, and which are not detailed in these regulations, are faithfully attended to.

85.   He must *see* that he has upon the train two sets of *signal flags, red lanterns,* and *red tail lamps,* a sufficient number of ordinary lanterns, spare shackles and pins, oil, tail rope, and detonating signals, &c.   He must see that he has *a signal cord properly connected,* and that he is provided with the customary papers, despatch bags and boxes.

86.   He will duly call the attention of the

repairer of cars, or of the station agent, in his absence, to any damage which may have been done to the cars, or to any which may come to his knowledge, that it may be promptly correct-ed, and he must notice these in his reports, as well as everything concerning the safety of the road and the requirements of the traffic.

87. It is his duty to *check the engine dri-vers* when they run unsafely, and to prescribe to them, when he sees fit, the regular rates allowed on the table, or slower rates if the track is in bad order.

88. He must not permit the sale of books, papers, or refreshments in the cars without per-mission from the commissioners.

89. He must not allow any passenger to ride on the platforms, or outside of the cars, nor to enter the baggage or freight cars.

90. He must prevent passengers endanger-ing themselves by imprudent exposure. In the event of any passenger being drunk or disorder-ly, to the annoyance of others, he must use all gentle means to stop the nuisance, failing which, he must exercise his authority and keep him in a separate place until he arrive at the next sta-tion, where the passenger must be left.

91. He must never make the *signal* for *starting* while passengers are getting aboard, and should, in making it, stand near to the front end of the front passenger car. He should then pass to the platform of the *last* car to see if any signals are made.

92. The conductor of a freight train has leisure on the road to examine the wheels, brakes and journals of his cars, and can have no excuse for allowing the journals to be neglected and become heated on the road. It will, therefore, always be presumed that the conductor is inattentive in regard to his subordinates, if the journals are neglected.

93. Conductors of freight trains must take no loaded cars without the proper *invoices*, nor *invoices* without the proper cars.

94. It is the duty of the conductor to require of the engine-driver *attention to the rules of the road.* Negligence or recklessness on the part of the engine-driver will be taken as a proof of the inefficiency of the conductor, unless such conduct has been duly and distinctly reported on every occasion of its taking place. He will at the same time treat the engine-driver with that consideration due to his very responsible duties, and will always advise with him in cases of difficulty.

95. In case of ACCIDENT TO A TRAIN, OR OF STOPPAGE ON THE MAIN LINE, from any cause, he must *immediately and always* station men with red flags or red lamps, and torpedoes in addition, if it be foggy, on each side of the track, at least half a mile from where the stoppage occurs; and he must do this, as a matter of course, *at all times and places ;* and he has *no right to assume* that there are no trains

approaching on either side of him. He will also, when assistance is wanted, or when the safety or convenience of the road requires it, send messengers to the station master on either side of him. Such masters must either personally notify all approaching trains, or place a man with the proper signal for that purpose. If the accident happen to a passenger train which has the right of the road, the conductor must immediately forward a written message by a trusty person, or by telegraph when it is available, to any other passenger train which will be in waiting; AND EVERY MAN EMPLOYED ON THE ROAD MUST ASSIST HIM IN FORWARDING THE SAID MESSAGE. He will also immediately telegraph or communicate with the Superintendent, who will instruct him what course to pursue. He may command the services of any freight, wood or gravel train or hand-car on the road, either to forward his own passengers, or to carry a message ; provided that he give no orders which shall interfere with the rights of other trains that may be on the road, without taking measures first to notify these trains, or to ensure their safety. He will take the best measures within his reach to have his train forwarded with the least possible delay, and every person in the neighborhood, in the employ of the Railway, is required to assist him. When the train is ready to proceed anew, the whistle signal shall be used to call in the men stationed out.

96. Great importance is attached to the

prompt delivery of letters, invoices, and despatches consigned to the care of the conductor.

97. He will see that the *doors* of *freight cars*, loaded with articles liable to be injured or stolen, are always *closed* and *locked*, and the doors of empty cars *closed*, and keep the *brakemen* at their posts. Whenever delay occurs at a station from *freight* being improperly stowed, he shall report the circumstances the same day to the Superintendent.

98. He will be held responsible for the safety of *live stock*, and will not allow them to be transported in close cars in warm weather. When there are any *horses* on a train, unless the owner has sent a person in charge of them, he will see that they are carefully watered and moderately fed on the road, if necessary, and such expense shall be paid him by the station master at the end of the journey.

99. It will be his duty to make himself acquainted, as far as is practicable, with the *condition* of the goods conveyed in the trains; and when they are so stowed as to be liable to damage, to change the stowage, or leave them at one of the stations, if necessary, to be forwarded more safely at another opportunity; also, at the end of his trip, to see that no pilfering of the contents of the cars has been committed.

100. Conductors will be held *personally responsible* for the proper care of all goods or property entrusted to them, while in their charge,

and will be careful to see that the same are delivered to the station masters according to the invoice.

101. It is his duty to attend to the removal of *empty cars* from sidings where they are not wanted, to the stations where they are wanted.

102. If, from any cause, it BECOMES NECESSARY TO LEAVE A CAR, or freight in any shape, where it does not belong, he shall note the facts on the back of the invoice, and give notice in writing to the station master where left, and to the Superintendent. He shall take all proper means to have the same forwarded to its destination without delay. In no case shall it remain over twenty-four hours, even if the conductor of another train be obliged to leave the same quantity from his train to take it; but perishable property must not be so left.

103. No conductor, brakeman, or other person, except the regular switchmen at stations, shall be permitted to unlock any switch thereat. At sidings where there are no switchmen, the conductor or engine-driver shall be the only persons authorized to unlock the switch, and the conductor is *responsible* that all *switches* are *left* in their *proper positions* after he has passed or used them.

104. Conductors will consider themselves to be, and act as, brakemen when necessary.

SECTION SIXTH.

Engine Drivers.

105. The engine-driver of every train must be in attendance half an hour before the appointed time for starting the train; and must see that his engine is in proper working order, sufficiently supplied with fuel, water, and properly oiled.

106. Every engine-driver shall have with him at all times in his tender the following tools :

A complete set of lamps ;
A complete set of screw keys ;
One traversing screw-jack ;
One common ditto and levers ;
One large and small monkey-wrench ;
Three cold chisels ; two hammers;
One pinch bar ; 5 short chains with hooks ;
A quantity of flax and twine ;
Four large and small oil cans;
Plugs for tubes and irons ;
Four fire buckets ;
Tackle and fall ;
Two sets of flags and 12 detonating signals ;
For which he will be *responsible*.

107. He must not *start his train* till directed by the conductor, nor till the bell be rung. He must answer the signal for *starting* by a

short *whistle* ; must invariably start with care, so as not to break the couplings, and see that he has the whole of his train before he gets beyond the limits of the station ; and he must run the train as nearly to time as possible, arriving at the stations neither too soon nor too late.

108. He shall allow no person to ride on his engine or tender, excepting the Commissioners, Superintendent, Engineer, or Road Master ; and he will be fined for every neglect of this rule.

109. He is to stand by the hand-gear, and keep a good look-out all the time that the engine is in motion. The fireman also is to keep a good look-out when not engaged in other duties.

110. He must cause the whistle to be sounded, where directed, at least one-fourth of a mile before arriving at any *public road crossing*, and to be continued until he pass it ; and the neglect of this precaution will be followed with immediate dismissal. He shall not pass any public road crossing at greater speed than five miles per hour.

111. He must sound the whistle with a continued sound, at *half a mile* from every station.

112. He must pass by stations where his train does not stop, at the rate of five miles per hour, and haul up where trains are receiving or discharging passengers.

113. When *attached to a train*, he will be subject to the order of the conductor, who has

exclusive charge of the train, and who will direct him when to start, when to stop, and what shifting of cars to make.

114. When *at a way station*, and not attached to a train, he will be subject to the orders of the station master.

115. He will be accountable for running off a switch *at any station where his train stops;* but he will not be held responsible for running off a switch at a station where his train does not stop. He will not pass over any switch at a greater speed than five miles per hour.

116. In *running behind another train*, he must so run as to allow the train in front of him to be at least three miles a-head when coming to stations, and, in approaching a station, or in running round or entering a curve, particular caution must be used to avoid the possibility of running into the leading train. NO EXCUSE WILL JUSTIFY THE SLIGHTEST NEGLECT OF THIS RULE.

117. He must keep a good look-out, as he moves forward, *for any signals*, or for any indication of danger, all of which he is *responsible for seeing* and immediately attending to; and he must obey any signal made by a repair man, or other person employed on the road, even if he should see reason to think such signal unnecessary. The lives of the passengers are entrusted to his care, and it is fully expected that he will not only attend to every signal, and to

all his instructions, but also that he will, *on all occasions*, be *vigilant* and *cautious* himself, not trusting alone to signals and rules for safety.

118. He must always run on the supposition that at any station he may find a train out of place, and he must have his *train well in hand* in approaching a switch or station.

119. Although the conductor has charge of the train, the engine-driver will *not* be consider-ed blameless if he run any unnecessary risk on the road without all the precautions being ob-served which are necessary to perfect safety ; nor will he be relieved from blame if he proceed in violation of the instructions or orders, even should the conductor, from negligence or mis-apprehension, direct him to do so.

120. He shall *not proceed* after *dark* with-out the *proper lights* on the front of his engine. If the proper lamps are out of order, he shall place in front of his engine common white lamps, which the conductor will furnish to him on ap-plication.

121. He is NEVER TO LEAVE HIS ENGINE IN STEAM without shutting the regulator, throw-ing the engine out of gear, and putting on the tender brakes.

122. He will not be allowed (except in cases of accident or sudden illness) to CHANGE his engine on the journey, nor to leave his station without permission.

123. He is strictly forbidden *throwing wood* or *waste*, or allowing the same to be done, from the tender while the train is in motion.

124. He must *start* and *stop* the train slowly, and without a jerk, which is liable to snap the couplings and chains. He must be careful not to shut off steam suddenly (except in case of danger), so as to cause a concussion of the cars.

125. The utmost care must be used in pushing cars into sidings, so as to avoid accidents.

126. In *bringing up the train*, he must pay particular attention to the state of the weather and the condition of the rails, as well as to the length of the train, and these circumstances must have due weight in determining when to shut off the steam. Stations must not be entered so rapidly as to require a violent application of the brakes, or to render the sounding of the signal whistle necessary. Every instance of overshooting the station must be reported to the Superintendent.

127. When passenger trains are behind time, he is *not at liberty to make it up*, but must keep to the rate of speed set forth in the timetable. It is equally wrong to be too soon as too late.

128. When a *conductor* is *disabled*, the engine-driver will have full charge of, and be held responsible for the safety of the train, until a proper person takes charge.

129. Before any train is backed into a siding or crossing, the conductor, fireman, or some competent person, must keep a good look out with a signal to stop any following train.

130. No engine is to run *tender or train foremost*, unless from unavoidable necessity, or by order of the Superintendent, and then only very slowly and to the nearest siding.

131. Speed must be slackened and the whistle constantly sounded in foggy weather. No ballast or wood engines must be on the line in a fog or snow storm.

132. Engine-drivers having charge of freight, ballast or wood trains must always *keep out of the way of passenger and special trains*, by shunting if necessary; and, if doubtful of getting out of the way, they must direct the repair man to make the usual signals to the following train, and to explain that a freight train is before them.

133. Engine-drivers with freight trains are to approach all stopping places at a speed not exceeding *ten miles* an hour when within *half a mile* of the stopping place, and to signal the brakeman to put on his brake before the tender brake is put on.

134. Engine-drivers in charge of freight trains must refuse to take cars of goods if they see that they are of a nature to take fire by a spark or hot cinder.

135. The targets of all switches must be perceived to be correct before they are passed.

136. Every engine-driver must carefully examine his engine *after each journey*, and he must immediately report any defect or deficiency in the engine or train to the Superintendent or foreman of locomotives.

137. He must report to the station master at the nearest station, and to the Superintendent, any accident, neglect, or irregular occurrence that he may have observed during the journey.

138. He must see that the signal cord is attached to the engine alarm bell before starting.

139. Engine-drivers must guard against killing stock. Should any animal be injured by the engine, the engine-driver must report the same in writing to the Superintendent, stating the facts of the case. Any engine-driver who neglects to make such a report immediately, will be held responsible for all the damages.

Table shewing the Speed of an Engine, when the time of performing a Quarter, Half, or One Mile is given.

Speed per hour.	Time of performing ¼ mile.	Time of performing half a mile.	Time of performing one mile.	Speed per hour.	Time of performing ¼ of a mile.	Time of performing half a mile.	Time of performing one mile.
Miles	m. s.	m. s.	m. s.	Miles	m. s.	m. s.	m. s.
5	3 0	6 0	12 0	23	0 39	1 18	2 36
6	2 30	5 0	10 0	24	0 37	1 15	2 30
7	2 8	4 17	8 34	25	0 36	1 12	2 24
8	1 52	3 45	7 30	26	0 34	1 9	2 18
9	1 40	3 20	6 40	27	0 33	1 6	2 13
10	1 30	3 0	6 0	28	0 32	1 4	2 8
11	1 21	2 43	5 27	29	0 31	1 2	2 4
12	1 15	2 30	5 0	30	0 30	1 0	2 0
13	1 9	2 18	4 37	31	0 29	0 58	1 56
14	1 4	2 8	4 17	32	0 28	0 56	1 52
15	1 0	2 0	4 0	33	0 27	0 54	1 49
16	0 56	1 52	3 45	34	0 26	0 53	1 46
17	0 52	1 46	3 21	35	0 25	0 51	1 43
18	0 50	1 40	3 20	36	0 25	0 50	1 40
19	0 47	1 34	3 9	37	0 24	0 48	1 37
20	0 45	1 30	3 0	38	0 23	0 47	1 34
21	0 42	1 25	2 51	39	0 23	0 46	1 32
22	0 40	1 21	2 43	40	0 22	0 45	1 30

SECTION SEVENTH.

Brakemen.

140. Brakemen must be at the starting station *one hour* before the departure of their train, get their lamps from station lamp room, clean and trim them, have their badges fixed on their caps, and be under the orders of the conductor.

141. Before starting, they must examine their brakes to see that they are in proper working order, and report any defect to the conductor. If with passenger trains, they shall see that their cars are carefully swept out and dusted, and (if necessary) the stoves lighted. and shall be very particular in seeing that wood, and that only of a proper size, is not put too near them. The wood must be piled carefully up under the seats, and not left in the passages. They shall have the lamps trimmed and ready for lighting, should their journey not be accomplished before dusk.

142. They must always ride *outside* the cars, so as to be in a position to apply their brakes immediately upon the signal being given by the engine-driver; and a *brakeman* and brake car shall always be *last* in the train.

143. Upon stopping at stations or sidings, brakesmen shall *examine the axle journals*, to see that none are heating; any seeming negligence in oiling to be reported.

144. Brakemen of all trains shall render every assistance in getting the cars marshaled at the station previous to starting, so that they may work their trains with greater despatch on the journey.

145. They shall give every assistance in wooding the engine of their train on the journey.

146. They shall see that a proper supply of

3

fresh water (which can be obtained at the stations) is always kept in the water coolers of the passenger cars.

SECTION EIGHTH.

Baggage Masters.

147. Baggage masters must be at the starting station one hour before the departure of the train, and are under the orders of the conductor. They will receive from passengers all baggage to be forwarded, and check or mark it plainly. Baggage must, in all cases, be handled with such care as to prevent injury, and all just cause of complaint.

148. Baggage checks must be kept at all times in a secure place, and they must not be exposed to theft or loss.

149. One hundred pounds of personal baggage will be allowed to each passenger, and all articles other than personal baggage, and all excess of personal baggage, will be charged for at double first class freight rates, and must be prepaid.

150. They will consider themselves to be, and will act as brakemen at all times.

SECTION NINTH.

Firemen.

151. Firemen are subject to the orders of the engine-driver while on their engines.

152. They will keep the engines cleaned and properly oiled, and assist the engine driver as may be required.

SECTION TENTH.

Mechanics and others in Workshops.

153. The ordinary working hours shall be from 7 till 6 o'clock; dinner hour from 12 to 1 o'clock.

In the morning, ten minutes will be allowed after the hour appointed (7 o'clock); if later than this, one half hour will be forfeited; if later than half-past 7 o'clock, one hour will be forfeited; and no admittance will be given after 8 o'clock.

Any workman being later than five minutes three times in one week will forfeit half an hour; five minutes will be allowed after 1 o'clock, P. M., but no admittance beyond this, without leave.

154. Every workman must commence his work and must not prepare to leave before the specified times.

155. Each workman, on entering the works, will be supplied with a time-book, having his name written upon it; and it must be carefully delivered to the time-keeper at the store every morning, with the time accurately entered for each job. These books will be returned in the evening.

156. Workmen absenting themselves without leave or sufficient reasons, shall not be allowed to resume work without permission from their respective foremen, and shall be liable to immediate dismissal.

157. Over-time will not be reckoned as such until sixty hours per week have been worked.

Men requiring to work at night will be paid time and quarter from 6 o'clock till 8 o'clock, and time and half from 8 o'clock till 6 o'clock, in the morning, allowing one hour and a half for refreshment. This will apply to any person sent out to work along the line; and when so sent, if he cannot return in the evening, he will be allowed a quarter of a dollar extra per day.

This rule only refers to mechanics.

158. Should any workman be detected taking from the works any copper, brass, wood, or other stores without authority, he will at once be handed over to the police authorities for punishment.

159. All tools given out to workmen will be entered by the storekeeper against the individual receiving them, who will be held responsible for their safe custody until the same is returned to the storekeeper after a job is finished, or when leaving the employment.

Any tools lost by carelessness or neglect will be replaced at the expense of the person losing them.

160. No workman allowed unnecessarily to be in any other part of the works than that in which his job is situated, or to talk to or interrupt other men at their work, under the penalty of immediate dismissal.

161. Smoking is strictly prohibited during working hours. All jobbing or making of any articles for private use at meal hours, as well as other times, is strictly prohibited. Any one found wasting stores or damaging jobs or tools wilfully will instantly be dismissed.

162. Spirituous or fermented liquors of every description not allowed within or on the works. Any one found with such in his possession, or in a state of intoxication, will be subject to immediate dismissal.

163. For the following offences any person will be liable to immediate dismissal :—

Any person neglecting to take to the store at once any old brass, copper, brass borings, or any other valuable material which may come into his hands.

Any person smoking during working hours.
Any person using a light, and not extinguishing it before leaving the works.

Any person picking tool chests or drawer locks, or taking another's tools without leave.

Any person passing into or out of the works by any other than the appointed entrance during working hours.

SECTION ELEVENTH.

Switchmen.

164.   The duties of switchmen require *care, attention,* and *watchfulness,* for any neglect may cause serious accidents.

165.   He must keep his switches clear and well oiled. Whenever a train has passed over, he will see that they are re-placed in the proper position, and kept locked. He must try his points before the passing through of any train.

166.   He *shall not,* when a train is due, or within fifteen minutes of the time, allow on any pretence an engine to pass from any siding on to the main line.

167.   He must always be furnished, when on duty, with the following articles :

1 hand signal lamp, having three colors, with oil and wick.

3 flags, white, red, and green.

168. He *must not* allow any engine to pass from one line to another without first ascertaining that it is safe to do so.

169. The switchman at the junction of the Windsor branch with the main line shall keep the danger signal always shown on the branch, and no engine-driver either on the main track or branch shall be allowed to approach within 300 yards of the junction, until he receives the proper signal to move forward.

SECTION TWELFTH.

Road Masters.

170. Road Masters will maintain a thorough inspection of the road, bridges, switches, crossings, culverts, drains, fences, and of everything pertaining to the safety of the road. He will have the charge and supervision of all repair men, and be held responsible for the faithful performance of their duty.

171. When materials are wanted for repairs, he will report to the Superintendent, as no bills will be allowed for purchases made other than by his order.

172. He must see that each gang of men is provided with two sets of signals, consisting of green, white, and red flags, a signal lamp and

oil, and with a time-table of the hours each train starts.

173. His duties are :—

To maintain the rails in proper gauge, perfect in line and level. and safe in all respects.

To remove all loose timber, stones, or iron from the road, and to keep the track clear from interruption of any kind.

To report to the Superintendent any defect in fences or any of the works.

To permit no gates to be left open or bars down longer than while in use.

To prevent all persons from trespassing on the railway, and, if necessary, to take such persons as persist in trespass into custody.

174. Every foreman shall walk over the portion of line under his charge every morning *before* the first train becomes due, for the purpose of examining the rails, chairs and side-keys, and the points and crossings, seeing there is no impediment in the way, nor materials lying between the rails, nor within three feet of either of them ; and that the road is in good order, and no danger to be apprehended to the passage of the engines or trains : and he shall prevent any train, by the proper signals, from passing along before this examination has been completed, and until he has assured himself that it is in safe running order. In cases where the road is under repair, or when circumstances may render it prudent, the foreman shall walk over his beat as often as may be necessary, or as he may be

directed by the road master, and he shall *not leave his beat until after the last regular train* has passed over it at night.

175. No broken chairs or other defective materials shall be permitted to remain on the road, but must be immediately removed; and when leaving at night, the men in squads shall deposit all the tools, &c., they have been using, under lock and key, in suitable places provided for this purpose.

176. The foreman shall not allow any waggon or car to be placed upon the road, nor any rail to be removed, nor temporary siding to be laid, without first obtaining special instructions from the road master, excepting in cases of emergency, and which must always be reported.

177. Ballast shall not be deposited between the rails, nor within three feet of either of them, at a greater height than three inches above their level. When engaged in this operation, great care must be taken to keep the stone and gravel clear of the rails.

178. The foreman shall see that no waggon left in any siding is nearer at any point than six feet from the main line, and that the choke blocks are fastened before the wheels.

179. This being a single line of railway, the points for the side roads require special care. The switch point, as a general rule, must always be *kept locked;* no dust or small stones shall be allowed to get between the switches and the

main rail; and all the working parts shall be properly oiled and made so as to move easily and smoothly.

180. The foreman shall report to the road master every accident that takes place on his beat—such as the failure of any of the works; and this must be done immediately by special messengers.

181. In cases of accident, the men in squads shall give every assistance in their power; and they shall obey the orders of the conductor in charge of the train in so doing.

182. When the road is under repair, the following signals must be shown to the engine-driver :—

If the road is safe, the man must stand on the side of the road holding the *white* flag or light.

If the road is in a rough state, the *green* flag or light should be shown, 200 yards on each side.

If a rail·is out, or from any other cause the road is dangerous, a man is to proceed at least 600 yards from the point of danger towards the approaching engine, and wave the *red* flag or *red* light.

183. No rail is to be raised more than *four inches* at one time, and this must be distributed over three rails' length. They must be firmly packed up *fifteen minutes* before the appointed time for the passing of any trains. The two

rails forming one line must be raised at the same time.

184. Nothing must be done on the track to make any impediment to the free transit of trains during a fog or snow-storm, except under urgent necessity.

185. Road masters, in their intercourse with the public and with landholders, will be civil and obliging, and endeavor to prevent injury to them or their property.

SECTION THIRTEENTH.

Private Road Crossings on the Level.

186. Owners or occupiers of ground to whom a level crossing has been granted shall provide suitable gates under lock and key.

187. Any person owning a crossing shall, before passing over it, be satisfied that the railway is clear, and no possibility of any accident.

188. If any person shall omit to shut and fasten any gate set up at either side of the railway for the accommodation of the owners or occupiers of the adjoining lands as soon as he and the carriage, cattle, or other animals under his charge have passed through the same, he shall forfeit for every such offence a sum not exceeding forty shillings.

189. The parties for whose accommodation

a crossing has been granted will be held responsible, and will be called upon to make good any damage that may be sustained.

SECTION FOURTEENTH.

Penalties.

190. Any servant of the Board transgressing or disobeying any of the foregoing regulations shall be liable to immediate dismissal, or a forfeiture of a month's pay and a fine of not more than five pounds.

191. All fines and forfeitures incurred under any regulation of the Board may be collected before any justice of the peace, or if within the city of Halifax, before the city courts, as an ordinary debt, and may be sued for in the name of any person entering the complaint, and the proceeds shall be paid into the general revenues of the province.

SECTION FIFTEENTH.

Regulations in regard to Passengers.

192. Passengers must procure tickets before taking their seats in the cars, subject to an increase of 1s. 3d. to the fare, in case of neglect, which the conductor will strictly enforce, except from stations where there is no ticket office.

193. Tickets are only good for the day on which they are issued.

194. Passengers must not smoke in the passenger cars or station houses, subject to a penalty of ten shillings for each offence.

195. They must not, under any circumstances, stand on the platforms of any cars when in motion, subject to a penalty of five shillings for each offence.

196. They must not go upon or leave the cars when in motion, nor put their heads or arms out of the car windows, subject to a penalty of five shillings for each offence.

197. Children will be charged for in the following proportions :—
Over twelve years of age, full price.
Between four and twelve years, half price.
Under four years, free.
The conductor will allow no person to travel free, unless under a pass from the Commissioners, Engineer, or Superintendent.

SECTION SIXTEENTH.

In regard to Baggage.

198. All baggage must be delivered to the baggage master or other person authorised to receive the same, before the passenger takes his seat in the cars.

199. Baggage must be accompanied *in the same train* by its owner. When not so accompanied, the railway will not be responsible in regard to it.

200. The liability of the railway, in regard to baggage and other articles transported upon a passenger train, will not commence till such baggage or other articles are received on board the train ; and such liability will terminate when such baggage or other articles are unladen from the train at their place of destination.

201. Baggage will not be taken to include money, merchandise, or other articles than those of personal use ; nor will the Commissioners be liable beyond the amount of twenty-five pounds currency for any single article of baggage.

202. The railway will not be liable for any baggage or article not given in charge to the baggage master, nor left at the stations for the convenience of the owner.

SECTION SEVENTEENTH.

General Notices and Conditions of Carriage.

203. The Commissioners will not be accountable for the safe carriage of any article or articles of freight unless receipted for by an authorized agent, nor will they be responsible, under any circumstances, to a greater amount upon

any single article of freight or passenger baggage than *twenty-five pounds* currency, unless upon notice being given of such amount, and special agreement made therefor.

204. The destination and name of consignee must be *plainly and distinctly marked* on all articles of freight, or no responsibility will be assumed for their miscarriage or loss.

205. The Commissioners will not be responsible for the loss of, or damage done to, money in cash, or bills, or promissory notes, or securities for money, or jewelry, trinkets, rings, bullion, precious stones, gold or silver, manufactured or unmanufactured, gold and silver plate, or plated articles, clocks, watches, time-pieces, marble, lace, furs, silks, in a manufactured or unmanufactured state, and whether wrought up or not wrought up with other materials; writings, title deeds, prints, paintings, maps, engravings, pictures, stamps, or other valuables; nor for damage done to china, glass, wearing apparel, musical instruments, furniture, toys, castings, or any other such hazardous or brittle articles, in packages or otherwise.

206. Nor for damages occasioned by delays from storms, accidents, or unavoidable causes, or for damages from the weather, fire, heat, frost, or decay of perishable articles, or from civil commotion.

207. Nor for loss or damage of any packages insufficiently or improperly packed, marked,

directed, or described, containing a variety of articles, liable, by breaking, to damage each other or other articles, nor for leakage, arising from bad casks or bad cooperage, or from fermentation.

208.   Nor for loss or damage done to goods put into returned wrappers, or boxes or packages described as empties; nor for any goods left until called for, or to order, warehoused for the convenience of the parties to whom they may belong, or by or to whom they are consigned.   Nor will they under any circumstances be accountable for loss or damage done to freight that is not taken away immediately after advice of arrival has been posted.

209.   Neither will they be responsible for any deficiency in weight or measure of grain, &c., in bags; nor for loss or deficiency in weight, number, or measure of lumber, &c., carried by the car load.

210.   No agent, or other employe of the Commissioners, is authorized to take charge of bank notes, money, or other valuable papers.

211.   Senders of any dangerous articles will be held accountable for any damage arising therefrom or thereto, unless the contents are described as such upon the direction, that due care may be observed in the loading; and in no case will the Commissioners be liable for the loss of any such articles; and they will not undertake the carriage of aquafortis, vitriol, friction

matches, or gunpowder, except by special agreement.

212. All articles will be at the risk of the owners, at the several Way Stations and places where Depot Buildings have not been established by the Commissioners, from the moment such articles are delivered, as directed or marked, or until taken into the Cars, as the case may be.

213. Fresh Fish, Meat and Poultry, Fruit or other perishable articles, are conveyed only at the owner's risk, and will immediately be sold to secure the Freight, if it be not paid when such articles arrive at the Railway Station, or are offered for delivery.

214. When Goods are intended, after being conveyed by this Railway, to be forwarded by some other company or conveyance to their final destination, the Duplicate Receipt furnished by the Consignor, must specify the same, and the articles be marked accordingly; the Commissioners will not be responsible for such articles after they are so delivered.

215. When an Invoice covers a variety of articles, as bales and boxes of Dry Goods, Furniture &c., each separate package must be properly marked and numbered, and a bill of particulars furnished by the Consignor, in duplicate, one to be receipted and the other to go with the Way Bill.

216. Storage will be charged on all Freight

4

remaining in the Depots over 48 hours after its arrival.

217. Demurrage at the rate of ten shillings per Car per day, will be charged on all cars not unloaded by Consignee, 24 hours after arrival, as per agreement, and the same must be paid before the goods are removed from the Station.

218. No claim for loss or damage (for which the Commissioners are accountable) will be allowed, unless notice in writing is given to the Station Freight Agent before the goods are removed from the Commissioners premises.

219. No less charge will be made for any single Package or Consignment than one shilling.

220. Live Stock must be fed by the owner or at his expense while in transit, and is taken entirely at his risk of loss, injury, damage, and all other contingencies, whether in loading, unloading, conveyance, or otherwise. When sent in quantities of less than one Car load, Live Stock will be charged for per head—to be prepaid in every case.

221. The charges on all Freight, &c., must be paid before the goods will be delivered; and the Commissioners do not hold themselves accountable for the correctness of any Monies charged as "back charges" on Freight, &c., by other Roads, Companies or individuals.

222. All Goods, from whomsoever received,

or to whomsoever belonging, are subject to a *Lien*, not only for the freight of the particular goods, but also for any general balance of freight that may be due from the Consignors, or Consignees,and if in fourteen days after the Commissioners have received the goods, the money due be not paid, they will be sold and the proceeds applied towards the satisfaction of such Lien and expenses.

223. Grain—Oats are estimated at 34 lbs. the bushel, Barley at 50 lbs., Wheat, Corn, and other Cerals at 60 lbs., per bushel. Flour, 200 lbs. per barrel.

224. Stone for building—12 cubic feet estimated at one ton.

Vehicles.

225. Vehicles will be taken as per schedule, at the owner's risk of damage from fire, the weather, and all other contingencies.

Live Stock.

226. *Per Car Load.*—For any distance not exceeding 20 miles, Thirty Shillings per Car Load, and One Shilling per Car Load per mile *additional* for all distances above 20 miles. Horned Cattle in less number than a Car Load, are charged *One penny per mile per head*, but no charge less than *One shilling and three pence ;* Sheep and Lambs are estimated at 90 lbs. and charged *Third class rates.* Calves and Swine are estimated at 150 lbs , and charged *Third class rates.* Dogs will be charged 1s. 3d. each, for any distance.

All Live Stock conveyed over this Railway are to be loaded and discharged by the owner or his agent, and to be under his sole care, and in all respects at his risk then, and during transit, also fed at his expense. One drover free, (second class) when accompanying his stock for the purpose of taking care of it, and paying the full price of a car load. Freight of all live stock to be prepaid.

Lumber and Timber.

227. For any distance not exceeding twenty miles, twenty shillings per car load. One shilling per car load per mile additional for all distances above twenty miles. No less charge will be made for any quantity than full car load.

A car load of soft wood boards, deals, or scantling, not to exceed 6,000 feet B. M.

A car load of hard wood boards, 4500f. B. M.

" logs or soft timber, 300 cubic ft.

" logs or hard timber, 250 "

Cord wood limited to six cords hard and eight cords soft wood per car load.

Pine, whitewood, basswood, hemlock, and spruce will be considered as *soft*, and all other kinds as *hard*. Loading and unloading to be done by owners and conveyed at their risk. Parties *overloading* will be charged *double rates* in every instance. Ship masts, and other long round timber, will be taken by special agreement only. Articles not named in the above, or in the classification, will be classed with analogous articles.

228. The Commissioners require the freight of all goods, lumber, &c., to be paid before delivery.

AN ACT FOR THE REGULATION OF RAILWAYS.

[Passed the 18th day of March, 1856.]

Be it enacted by the Governor, Council, and Assembly, as follows :—

1. If any person shall wilfully obstruct any persons acting under the authority of the Commissioners, in the lawful exercise of their power, in setting out the line of the Railway, or shall pull up or remove any poles, pegs, or stakes driven into the ground for the purpose of so setting out the line of the Railway, or shall deface or destroy any pegs or marks put down or made for the same purpose, or shall wilfully obstruct any of the contractors, or their servants or workmen, while employed in the construction of the Railway, he shall forfeit a sum not exceeding five pounds for every such offence.

2. If any person shall wilfully obstruct the

passing of any engine or carriage along the road, or shall maliciously place anything on the Railroad calculated to obstruct the passage of any engine or carriage, or to injure or endanger the same, or shall maliciously injure the Railroad or anything thereto appertaining, or any materials or implements for the construction or use thereof, or any of the property in the possession or under the control of the Commissioners as such, he shall be guilty of felony, and be imprisoned in the penitentiary for a term not exceeding fourteen years.

3. If any person shall wilfully obstruct or impede any officer, servant, or agent of the Commissioners, in the execution of his duties upon the Railway, or upon or in any of the stations or other works or premises connnected therewith, or if any person shall wilfully trespass upon the Railway, or any of the stations or other works or premises connected therewith, and shall refuse to quit the same upon request to him made by any officer, servant or agent of the Commissioners, or shall wilfully disturb, break down, injure or destroy any of the fences of the Railway, or remove the same or any part thereof, or shall blot out or deface any regulations put up upon the line, or pull down or injure the boards upon which such regulations are affixed,—every such person so offending, and all others aiding or assisting therein, shall severally forfeit a sum not exceeding twenty-five pounds for every such offence.

4. If any person shall omit to shut and fasten any gate set up at either side of the Railway, for the accommodation of the owners or occupiers of the adjoining lands, as soon as he and the carriage, cattle, or other animals under his care have passed through the same, he shall forfeit for every such offence a sum not exceeding forty shillings.

5. If any person, after the Railroad, or any section thereof, shall be opened for use, shall himself go thereon, or shall drive or lead any animal thereon, he shall for every such offence forfeit a sum not exceeding forty shillings ; but nothing in this regulation shall prevent the passing across the Railroad where the same is crossed by any other road on a level therewith.

6. If any animal shall be found going at large within the limits of the Railroad, or any section thereof, after the same shall be opened for use, the owner thereof, and the person through whose default or neglect the same shall occur, shall for every such offence severally forfeit a sum not exceeding forty shillings, provided the Railroad shall have on the sides thereof, where it does not cross some other road on the same level, a fence approved of by the Commissioners.

7. If any person shall travel or attempt to travel in any carriage belonging to the railroad, without having previously paid his fare, and with intent to avoid payment thereof, or if any

person having paid his fare for a certain distance knowingly and wilfully proceed in any such carriage beyond such distance without previously paying the additional fare for the additional distance, and with intent to avoid payment thereof, or if any person knowingly and wilfully refuse or neglect, on arriving at the point to which he has paid his fare, to quit such carriage, or if any person while in such carriage shall offend or annoy the other passengers therein by riotous conduct, or by indecent or profane language, or shall disobey the lawful directions of the guard, or shall persist in smoking after a request from the guard or from any other passenger to desist therefrom, every such person shall for every such offence forfeit a sum not exceeding five pounds.

8. If any person be discovered either in or after committing or attempting to commit any such offence as in the preceding regulation mentioned, all officers and servants of the Commissioners, and such other persons as they may call to their aid, and all constables, gaolers, and peace officers, may lawfully apprehend and detain such person until he can conveniently be taken before some justice, or until he can be otherwise discharged in due course of law.

9. If any person shall send by the Railway any aquafortis, oil of vitriol, gunpowder, lucifer matches, or other goods of a dangerous character, without distinctly marking their nature on the outside of the package containing the same,

or otherwise giving notice to the book-keeper or other servant of the Commissioners with whom the same are left at the time of so sending, he shall forfeit for every such offence a sum not exceeding twenty pounds.

10. It shall be lawful for the Commissioners to make and levy such tolls as in their opinion shall be best adapted for the accommodation of the traffic, and to alter and vary the same from time to time, as they may see fit; provided that all such tolls be at all times charged equally to all persons, and after the same rate, whether per tón, per mile, or otherwise, in respect of all passengers, and of all goods or carriages of the same description, and conveyed or propelled by a like carriage or engine passing only over the same portion of the line of Railway under the same circumstances.

11. The tolls shall be paid to such persons, and at such places, and in such manner, and under such regulations as the Commissioners shall appoint.

12. If on demand any person fail to pay the tolls due in respect of any carriage or goods, it shall be lawful for the Commissioners to detain and sell such carriage, or all or any part of such goods; or if the same shall have been removed from the premises of the Railway, to detain and sell any other carriages or goods within such premises belonging to the party liable to pay such tolls, and out of the money arising from

such sale to retain the tolls payable as aforesaid, and all charges and expenses of such detention and sale, rendering the overplus, if any, to the person entitled thereto ; or it shall be lawful for the Commissioners to recover any such tolls by action at law.

13. If any person being the owner or having the care of any carriage or goods passing or being upon the railway, shall on demand fail to give to any person appointed to collect the tolls, a true and correct account in writing signed by him of the number and quantity of goods conveyed by any such carriage, and of the point on the Railway from which such carriage or goods have set out, or are about to set out, and at what point the same are to be unloaded or taken off the Railway, and if the goods conveyed by any such carriage, or brought for conveyance as aforesaid, be liable to payment of different tolls, shall fail to specify the respective quantities or numbers thereof liable to each or any such tolls, with intent to avoid in any case the payment thereof, he shall for every such offence forfeit and pay to the Commissioners a sum not exceeding ten pounds for every ton of goods, or for any parcel not exceeding one hundred weight, and so on in proportion for any quantity of goods less than one ton, or for any parcel exceeding one hundred weight (as the case may be) which shall be upon any such carriage, and such penalty shall be in addition to the toll to which such goods may be liable.

14. If any passenger shall wilfully cut the lining, or remove or damage any part of the carriages, or shall get into or get off of any train when in motion, or at any other place than the passengers' platform, or attempt to do so, every such person shall for every such offence forfeit and pay a sum not exceeding forty shillings.

15. Passengers at the road stations will only be booked conditionally, that is to say, in case there shall be room in the train for which they are booked. If there shall not be room for all so booked, the passengers for the longer distance will be allowed the preference, and for the same distance they will have priority according to the number of their tickets.

16. The owners of goods and property of every description conveyed by the Railway, liable to injury from the weather, or from smoke sparks or fire, shall be responsible for their proper protection, unless under a special bargain with the Commissioners.

17. If any person shall load any carriage on the Railway so that the loading extends more than two feet beyond the flange of the wheels, or shall leave any carriage or goods or things under his charge to remain on the Railway, or in any of the depots or sidings thereof, to an obstruction of the working of the Railway, every such person for every such offence shall forfeit and pay a sum not exceeding forty shillings.

18. If any person convicted under any of the preceding sections, shall not pay the judgement and costs, and no goods can be found whereon to levy the same, such person may be imprisoned in the common jail of the county for a term not exceeding one day for every five shillings of the amount of the judgment, provided such term shall in no case exceed three months.

THE foregoing Rules and Regulations were made by the Board of Commissioners.

JAMES McNAB,
Chairman.

Confirmed by the Governor in Council,
June 3rd, 1859.